Meet
BABAR
and His Family

Laurent de Brunhoff

Abrams Books for Young Readers
New York

Designer, Abrams Edition: Edward Miller

The artwork for each picture is prepared using watercolor on paper.
This text is set in 13-point Comic Sans.

Library of Congress Cataloging-in-Publication Data:

Brunhoff, Laurent de.
Meet Babar and his family / Laurent de Brunhoff.
p. cm.
Summary: Babar and his family enjoy a variety of activities during each season of the year.
ISBN 0-8109-0555-8
[1. Elephants—Fiction. 2. Seasons—Fiction.] I. Title.
PZ7.B82843 Me 2002
[E]—dc21
2001005349

Printed and bound in Belgium
10 9 8 7 6 5 4

HNA
harry n. abrams, inc.
a subsidiary of La Martinière Groupe
115 West 18th Street
New York, NY 10011
www.hnabooks.com

Meet
BABAR
and His Family

One morning Babar, the king of the elephants, opens his windows. It is a sunny day in Celesteville. The birds are chirping. The leaves and flowers seem to have opened overnight. Babar is happy. "It's spring!" he shouts. "It's spring!"

Babar's wife, Queen Celeste, and their three children—Pom, Flora, and Alexander—are already outside enjoying the beautiful day.

Babar joins Celeste by the lake. Birds have built their nests in all the trees and bushes. They are bringing food to feed to their babies, who open their beaks wide.

In the spring the children like to play outdoors. Babar's young cousin, Arthur, is riding his bicycle with his friend Zephir the monkey.

Babar buys some delicious cakes at the bakery and takes them to his good friend the Old Lady. What a surprise! Cornelius, the oldest of the elephants, is there for tea.

During the summer Babar works hard in his garden. He waters the flowers faithfully. The children help him—in their own way. That rascal Arthur loves to play tricks!

On a very hot day what fun it is to eat ice-cream cones!

The children like to watch Babar and Celeste play tennis. The ball goes *p-o-c-k!* against their tennis rackets.

Babar and Celeste often give big parties for their friends in the Celesteville gardens.

Sometimes Babar and Celeste go sailing. They glide silently over the cool water.

Later, Flora asks her father to take the family
for a drive through the countryside.

The elephants gather around the Celesteville bandstand for the last concert of the summer.

Suddenly rain pours down. What a pity! Everyone has to run for cover.

Now autumn has come. The Old Lady goes for a walk with Babar and Cornelius. "How I love to go walking when the leaves are red and gold!" she exclaims.

The school bus picks up Pom, Flora, and Alexander for their first day of school.

The Old Lady is their teacher. She is not at all strict.

In the winter the Babar family goes ice-skating. Babar and Celeste skate gracefully to the music. But Pom and Alexander try to skate as fast as Arthur.

Pom falls and hurts his knee. Celeste calls Doctor Capoulosse right away. "This is not too serious," he says.

Pom's cut heals by the time the family goes to the mountains to ski. At the railroad station, Zephir calls, "Quick! The train is going to leave!"

When they arrive, they take a funny little car that goes straight up the steep slope to the top of the mountain. Everything is covered with snow. Even the evergreens are white.

Babar enters the ski-jump contest. The children watch as he soars off the ski jump, flying like a bird. "When I am big, I will jump, too," Arthur thinks.

The next day snow falls in huge flakes. No skiing now. It is a good day for a snowball fight! The children make a snowman. Who does he look like?

The Babar family returns to Celesteville in time for the new year.
Pom, Flora, and Alexander stand by the window, watching the moon
shine over the whole countryside.